THE
TOPSY-TURVY
STORYBOOK

By the same author

ACE · ALPHABEASTS · DAGGIE DOGFOOT
THE FOX BUSTERS · HARRY'S MAD · THE JENIUS
MAGNUS POWERMOUSE · MARTIN'S MICE
THE MOUSE BUTCHER · NOAH'S BROTHER
THE QUEEN'S NOSE · SADDLEBOTTOM
THE SHEEP-PIG *(Winner of the Guardian Award for Children's Fiction 1984)*
SUPER TERRIFIC PIGS · THE TOBY MAN · TUMBLEWEED

First published in Great Britain 1992 by Victor Gollancz Ltd, 14 Henrietta
Street, London WC2E 8QJ   Text copyright © Fox Busters Ltd 1992
Illustrations © John Eastwood 1992   The right of Dick King-Smith and
John Eastwood to be identified as authors of this work has been asserted
by them in accordance with the Copyright, Designs and Patents Act 1988
A catalogue record for this book is available from the British Library
ISBN 0 575 05429 8   Typeset by Cameron Typesetting Ltd,
Printed in Great Britain by Cambus Litho Ltd

DICK KING-SMITH

THE TOPSY-TURVY STORYBOOK

with illustrations by

JOHN EASTWOOD

LONDON · VICTOR GOLLANCZ LTD · 1992

Contents

Bear and the Three Goldilocks 7

Thinderella 11

There Was an Old Woman 17

Rapunzel 18

Ding, Dong, Bell 19

Little Miss Muffet 19

The Wolf and the Seven Little Kids 20

Hickory, Dickory, Dock 22

The Queen of Hearts 22

The Ugly Duckling 23

Georgie Porgie 26

Pat-a-Cake 27

Pop Goes the Weasel 27

A Muddy Great Puddle 28

Huge Red Riding Hood 31

Humpty Dumpty 33

Little Jack Horner — 34

Jack Sprat — 34

The Princess and the P (for Pumpkin) — 35

Hansel and Gretel — 38

Jack and Jill — 41

Mary Had a Little Lamb — 41

Diddle Diddle Dumpling — 42

Simple Simon — 42

George Washington — 43

Snow-White — 45

King Canute — 51

Mary, Mary — 53

Little Bo-Peep — 53

The Frog King — 54

Robin Hood and his Miserable Men — 56

Rock-a-bye, Baby — 60

Ring-a-ring o'Roses — 60

The Sleeping Beauty — 61

I Love Little Pussy — 64

BEAR AND THE
THREE GOLDILOCKS

There were once three sisters, triplets they were, as like as three peas in a pod, and all called Goldilocks.

This was partly because they all had golden hair, and partly because their mother was too stupid and lazy to choose different names for them so she called them Goldilocks One, Goldilocks Two and Goldilocks Three.

When the three Goldilocks grew up, they left home and set up house together in a forest.

In the forest there lived a bear, called, quite simply, Bear.

One day the three Goldilocks left on a visit to their stupid lazy old mother, and while they were away, Bear came out of the trees and into their house.

Inside he found three identical beds, three identical chairs and three identical bowls of porridge.

Bear lay on the three beds in turn and smashed the lot.
Then he sat on the three chairs in turn and splintered the lot.
Then he tried the three bowls of porridge in turn and scoffed the lot.

Then he heard the three Goldilocks coming back, so, still feeling very hungry, he hid and listened.

"Look!" said Goldilocks One. "Someone's bust our beds!"

"Look!" said Goldilocks Two. "Someone's crushed our chairs!"

"Look!" said Goldilocks Three. "Someone's polished off our porridge!"

After that they never said another word, ever again.

I expect you can guess why.

If not, I can't bear to tell you.

THINDERELLA

Once upon a time there was a tall skinny girl named Thinderella.

Her arms were like sticks and her legs were like walking-sticks and an ordinary-sized dog-collar would have fitted round her middle with no trouble at all. She also had very big feet.

Thinderella had two older sisters called Gwendoline and Mirabelle, and they were as beautiful as she was plain. Handsome girls they were, with plenty of flesh on their bones, not fat but well-rounded. Buxom, you would have called them.

Gwendoline had long straight hair as black as a raven's wing, and Mirabelle had long curly hair as golden as ripe corn, and people called them the Lovely Sisters.

Thinderella's hair was short and mousy, and no one ever said anything nice about her.

"Scruffy thing!" they said. "And so scrawny too! It's hard to believe she's related to the Lovely Sisters. Why, she goes about in rags, and barefoot too!"

The reason for this was simple. Gwendoline and Mirabelle spent lavishly upon themselves, buying all manner of expensive clothes, but they did not even allow Thinderella pocket-money. Not that she had any pockets to put it in. All she got was the leftovers of food that the Lovely Sisters couldn't manage, just enough to give her the strength to do the cooking and the cleaning and the washing and the ironing and the mending.

One day a letter arrived addressed to the Misses Gwendoline and Mirabelle. It was an invitation to a Grand Ball, to celebrate the twenty-first birthday of Prince Hildebrand, the son of the King of that country.

"Look!" said Gwendoline, flourishing it under Thinderella's pinched little nose.

"But don't touch!" said Mirabelle. "Your hands are filthy."

"I've been doing the fires," said Thinderella.

"Well, go and wash," said Gwendoline.

"And then you can help us on with our best clothes," said Mirabelle. "So that we can go downtown."

"And buy some even better ones for the Ball."

When the great night came, and the Lovely Sisters had set off for the Ball, sumptuously dressed and glittering with jewellery, Thinderella sat by the kitchen fire, staring sadly at the glowing embers.

"How I wish I could go to the Ball," she whispered softly, and two big tears ran down her grimy cheeks.

"So you shall!" said a voice.

Thinderella looked round to see a strange little man sitting cross-legged on the kitchen table. He had very long hair and a big moustache and a bushy beard, so that all Thinderella could see of his face was a red nose and a pair of twinkling eyes.

"Who are you?" she said.

"I," said the little man, "am your Hairy Godfather, and you *shall* go to the Ball. Run off and have a good wash, Thinders, and put some clean clothes on."

"But I haven't any," said Thinderella.

"You'll be surprised," said the Hairy Godfather, and sure enough when she reached her dark attic room, there was a ball-gown laid out ready on the bed.

Quickly Thinderella washed herself, especially her feet which were very big and flat through always going about barefoot, and she put on the gown. But, she thought, I have no shoes, and then she looked under the bed and there was a pair of very large slippers, made all of glass. And she tried them on and they fitted perfectly.

Hastily Thinderella combed her short mousy hair with her newly-cleaned fingers and went downstairs again.

"Not bad," said her Hairy Godfather. "The gown's a bit plain, but it'll do."

"But please," said Thinderella, "I'm a bit plain too. Prince Hildebrand is sure to dance the night away with Gwendoline and Mirabelle but he'll never look twice at me."

"You'll be surprised," said the Hairy Godfather. "Now then, got a pumpkin about the place?"

"No."

"Got any mice?"

"Mice? What for?"

"Oh forget it," said the Hairy Godfather. "It won't take you long to walk. It's not far and it isn't raining. Have a good time. Oh, and by the way, don't stay there after midnight."

In fact, walking even a short distance in glass slippers is murder on the feet, and by the time Thinderella arrived at the Palace, hers were agony. She hobbled into the ballroom and flopped down on a chair and stuck her thin legs out and wriggled her toes inside the glass slippers.

At that moment a young man who was walking by fell over her enormous great feet.

"Oh sorry!" gasped Thinderella.

"My fault," said the young man. "I wasn't looking where I was going," and indeed Thinderella could see that he wore very thick spectacles.

"By the way," he said, "my name's Hildebrand," and he stuck out a hand, vaguely in her direction.

"Oh!" she said. The Prince, she thought. He's not very handsome and he's *very* short-sighted, but he's got ever such a nice smile.

"Happy birthday," she said.

"Oh, thanks a lot," said the Prince.

She's got ever such a nice voice, he thought.

"I won't ask you to dance," he said. "I'm so clumsy, I'm always treading on people's feet."

"You would on mine," said Thinderella. "They're huge," and she took off one glass slipper and gave it to him.

"Have a look at that," she said.

Just then Gwendoline and Mirabelle came by in all their finery, and their lovely eyes positively bulged at the sight of their sister, neatly dressed and talking to the Prince. But before they could open their lovely mouths, the clock began to strike.

"Oh gosh!" cried Thinderella. "Midnight!" And she dashed away, leaving Prince Hildebrand holding one of the glass slippers.

In fact the clock was only striking ten, and when she got home, her Hairy Godfather was still sitting on the kitchen table, eating pickled gherkins.

"Hello, Thinders," he said. "You're early. What happened? Didn't the Prince look twice at you?"

"Oh more than that," said Thinderella. "He's very short-sighted, you see. But he's ever so nice, Hairy Godfather. I'm so glad I went to the Ball."

"Good," said the Hairy Godfather. "And goodnight," and he disappeared.

When Thinderella woke up next morning the ball-gown and the remaining glass slipper had disappeared too, so she got up to do the housework in her usual ragged clothes. She made breakfast for the Lovely Sisters and took it up to them.

They were furious with her.

"What were you doing at the Ball?" shouted Gwendoline.

"And where did you get that gown?" yelled Mirabelle.

"And what d'you think you were doing chatting up the Prince?" they both screamed.

At that moment there was a knock at the front door.

Thinderella ran down and opened it and there stood Prince Hildebrand, holding the other glass slipper and peering at her with his weak eyes through his thick spectacles.

"Is there anyone here whose foot will fit this slipper?" he said, coming in and tripping over the mat. "If so, I will marry her."

The Lovely Sisters, who had been leaning over the banisters listening, came rushing down the stairs crying "It's mine! It's mine!" but of course when they tried it on in turn, it was far too big for their lovely little feet.

But when Thinderella put her great beetle-crusher in the slipper, it fitted perfectly!

"I told you," she said to the Prince. "They're huge. Don't you remember?"

How could I forget that nice voice, thought Prince Hildebrand, and he smiled his nice smile and put out his hand, vaguely in Thinderella's direction.

"I'm offering you this hand in marriage," he said. "Will you take it?"

And Thinderella took it, while the Lovely Sisters hurried away, their lovely faces contorted with jealous rage. So angry were they that they did not notice a little man with very long hair and a big moustache and a bushy beard, sitting cross-legged under the staircase, and grinning all over his face, or as much of it as could be seen.

The short-sighted Prince of course did not notice either, but Thinderella saw him and they winked at one another.

"By the way," said Prince Hildebrand as his betrothed helped him down the front steps, "I don't even know your name?"

"It's Thinderella," said Thinderella.

"What a perfectly beautiful name," said the Prince, blinking at her through his thick spectacles, "for a perfectly beautiful girl."

THERE WAS AN OLD WOMAN

There was an old woman
Who lived in a trainer,
She'd so many children
They drove her insaner.
She got a good price
For a few of the best,
And took seven pounds
Fifty pence for the rest.

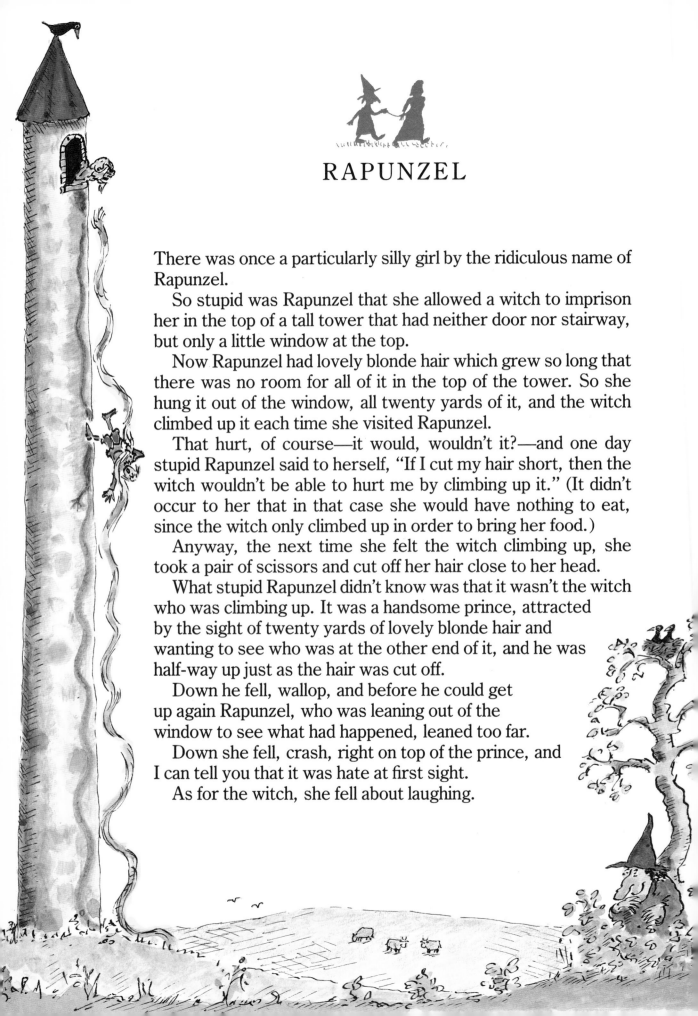

RAPUNZEL

There was once a particularly silly girl by the ridiculous name of Rapunzel.

So stupid was Rapunzel that she allowed a witch to imprison her in the top of a tall tower that had neither door nor stairway, but only a little window at the top.

Now Rapunzel had lovely blonde hair which grew so long that there was no room for all of it in the top of the tower. So she hung it out of the window, all twenty yards of it, and the witch climbed up it each time she visited Rapunzel.

That hurt, of course—it would, wouldn't it?—and one day stupid Rapunzel said to herself, "If I cut my hair short, then the witch wouldn't be able to hurt me by climbing up it." (It didn't occur to her that in that case she would have nothing to eat, since the witch only climbed up in order to bring her food.)

Anyway, the next time she felt the witch climbing up, she took a pair of scissors and cut off her hair close to her head.

What stupid Rapunzel didn't know was that it wasn't the witch who was climbing up. It was a handsome prince, attracted by the sight of twenty yards of lovely blonde hair and wanting to see who was at the other end of it, and he was half-way up just as the hair was cut off.

Down he fell, wallop, and before he could get up again Rapunzel, who was leaning out of the window to see what had happened, leaned too far.

Down she fell, crash, right on top of the prince, and I can tell you that it was hate at first sight.

As for the witch, she fell about laughing.

DING, DONG, BELL

Ding, dong, bell,
Johnny's in the well!
Who was it did that?
Our old pussy-cat.
Will she pull him out?
Never, though he shout.
What a clever cat she's been
To try to drown that Johnny Green,
Who always meant to do her harm
And teased and chased her round the farm.

LITTLE MISS MUFFET

A whopping great spider
With four flies inside her
Was eating a fifth on a tuffet,
When suddenly coshed
And disgustingly squashed
By a fat little girl called Miss Muffet.

19

THE WOLF AND THE SEVEN LITTLE KIDS

Every mother knows that it's quite wrong to go out of the house and leave her kids unattended. But there was once a nanny-goat foolish enough to do just that.

Off she went, leaving her seven kids behind. What's more, she must have known there was a wolf about, because she warned them not to open the door.

But when she returned, she found that the wolf had indeed called at her house. He'd fooled the kids into letting him in and then he'd scoffed the lot. Except one, the smallest, who'd hidden inside the grandfather clock.

Well now, this dumb nanny-goat had a really nutty idea. "Get some scissors and a needle and thread," she said to the smallest kid.

"Why, Mum?" said the smallest kid.

"It's simple," said the nanny-goat. "We'll find the wolf asleep. We'll cut him open and out will pop your six brothers and sisters. Then we'll fill his belly up with stones and sew him up again."

"Why, Mum?" said the smallest kid.

"Use your brains," said his mother. "When the wolf wakes up, he'll be thirsty, and he'll go to the river and topple in and drown."

"Why, Mum?" said the smallest kid.

"Because of the weight of the stones inside him, of course."

The nanny-goat was right about the first bit. They did find the wolf asleep.

But (as you might expect) the very first touch of the point of the scissors on his stomach woke him up sharply.

He swallowed the smallest kid in one gulp.

Then he said to the nanny-goat, "I should have thought you would have known that it's quite wrong to go out of the house and leave your kids unattended?"

"I do! I do!" bleated the nanny-goat. "I'll never do it again as long as I live!"

"Which is no time at all," said the wolf, licking his chops.

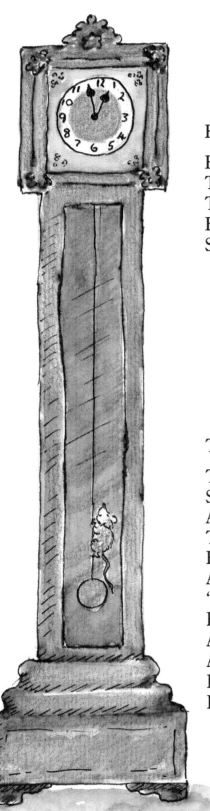

HICKORY, DICKORY, DOCK

Hickory, dickory, dock,
The mouse got in the clock;
The unfortunate thing
Became caught in the spring,
Squishery, squashery, shplock!

THE QUEEN OF HEARTS

The Queen of Hearts
She made some tarts,
All jammy, fresh and hot.
The Knave of Hearts
He stole those tarts
And scoffed the blooming lot.
"How very mean,"
Remarked the Queen,
And vowed no more to bake.
As for the Knave,
His feasting gave
Him dreadful tummy-ache.

THE UGLY DUCKLING

An ordinary farmyard duck once hatched out a brood of ordinary ducklings. But when they were all free of their eggshells and scuttering about as newborn ducklings do, there was still one egg left in the nest.

It was a much bigger egg than the others had been, and the duck continued doggedly to sit upon it, hoping that it, too, would hatch. Which, some days later, it did.

Soon the duck could see that this last child was unlike his brothers and sisters. He was larger, he was greyish where they were yellow, and his legs and feet were bigger and his neck much longer than theirs.

The duck thought him quite beautiful, and, proud mother that she was, she constantly told him so.

"You, my son," she said, day in, day out, "are beautiful. Your brothers and sisters are healthy normal ordinary ducklings, but you alone are beautiful," and she constantly showed him off to the other birds in the farmyard, the hens and the geese and the turkeys.

"Look at him," the old duck said to them, day in, day out. "Is he not the most beautiful duckling you ever set eyes on?"

Not surprisingly, after all this constant flattery, the beautiful duckling grew up to be extremely big-headed.

He would stand by the duck pond and look at his reflection and say to himself, "Observe my noble body and my powerful wings and my great webbed feet and my long and elegant neck. What a truly beautiful duckling I am!"

And at last, to cap it all, his plumage which had been grey turned to a brilliant snowy whiteness.

One day the beautiful duckling left the duck pond and made his way to a nearby lake. Here he stood by the water's edge and looked once more at his reflection.

"Without doubt," he said, "I must be the most beautiful duckling in the world. No other could compare with me."

Then he looked up and saw a whole flock of great white birds swimming on the surface of the lake, birds that looked just like him, birds that certainly could compare with him.

"Even so, they cannot be as beautiful as I," he said to himself, and he swam proudly out to meet them.

At sight of this stranger approaching the swans banded together, arching their wings and hissing angrily.

"Who are you?" they cried, and the reply came "Make way! I am the beautiful duckling."

"Duckling!" said one of the swans to the rest, and "He's mad!" said another. "And he's a big-head!" said a third, and then a host of voices said, "Let's duck the duckling!"

And with that all the swans set upon the newcomer.

They buffeted him with their wings, and pecked at him, and pulled out his tail feathers, and finally they ducked his head under water.

Somehow, he struggled back to the duck pond, and saw the old duck who had hatched him so long ago but now did not recognise the battered, muddied bird, his neck limp, his wings trailing, his plumage all in dirty disarray.

"Who on earth are you?" she said.

"The beautiful duckling!" he gasped.

"A duckling you may be," said the old duck doubtfully, "but beautiful you are not. Sure as eggs is eggs, there's only one word to describe you. Ugly!"

GEORGIE PORGIE

Georgie Porgie, sloppy and sly,
Kissed the girls and made them cry;
But when all the boys came out,
It was Georgie's turn to shout.

PAT-A-CAKE

Pat-a-cake, pat-a-cake, baker's man,
Bake me a cake as rich as you can;
Ice it and slice it and serve it up hot,
And don't you tell Tommy 'cos I want the lot.

POP GOES THE WEASEL

Half a pound of tuppenny rice,
Half a pound of treacle.
Finish off with five fat mice,
BURP! goes the weasel.

A MUDDY GREAT PUDDLE

Queen Elizabeth the First, who was a very bossy lady, went on a visit to Tilbury to inspect her fleet.

She was accompanied by a number of her gentlemen, including Sir Walter Raleigh, who was a very fussy man.

It was a rainy day, as Sir Walter tittupped along behind the Queen. He was very particular about his clothes and he did not want to get his shoes wet.

Suddenly, rounding a corner, they came upon a muddy great puddle that stretched right across the path.

Queen Elizabeth stopped and turned to Sir Walter Raleigh.

"Sir Walter," she said. "Pray spread your cloak across yonder muddy great puddle so that I may cross it dry-shod."

Sir Walter was horrified. His cloak was a fine new one, of richest velvet lined with fur, and the last thing he wanted was to chuck it into a lot of dirty water.

I'm not falling for that, he thought. But he was wrong.

Queen Elizabeth, seeing him hesitate, gave him such a shove in the back that he fell flat on his face in the muddy great puddle with an almighty splash. Then the Queen walked across him, followed in turn by her other gentlemen.

When the last one had used this human bridge, they turned to see Sir Walter Raleigh rise from the muddy great puddle, soaked to the skin and dripping wet, looking in fact like a drowned rat.

"Odsbodikins!" cried the Queen to the others. "We shall have to change his name."

"What shall you call him, Majesty?" they said.

"Sir Water," said Queen Elizabeth, and everyone burst out laughing.

Except Sir Walter Raleigh.

HUGE RED RIDING HOOD

There was once an enormous great lump of a girl called Huge Red Riding Hood. One day she set out to visit her grandmother, who lived alone in a little cottage in the woods.

Huge Red Riding Hood was carrying a basket of goodies for the old lady, but somehow before long the basket was empty. Huge Red Riding Hood rubbed her huge stomach.

"That's better!" she said.

Just then a wolf appeared and gazed at her hungrily. He thought of saying "Hullo, little girl", but she obviously wasn't so he said, "Hullo, huge girl" instead.

"Hi," said Huge Red Riding Hood, wiping her mouth on the back of her hand.

"And where are you going?" said the wolf.

"To visit my grandmother."

"And where does she live?" asked the wolf.

I'll get there first, he thought, and gobble the old lady up. Then I'll get into bed and pretend to be her and when this huge girl turns up I'll have her for afters.

But Huge Red Riding Hood knew just what he was thinking, and she directed him to her grandmother's cottage by a long, roundabout route. Then she took a short cut and got there first.

"Hullo, dear," said her grandmother. "I see you've brought me a basket of goodies."

"Don't worry about that, Gran," said Huge Red Riding Hood. "There's a wolf on his way."

"But I'm hungry."

"So's he," said Huge Red Riding Hood. "You get in the cupboard and keep quiet," and she shoved the old lady inside and locked the cupboard door.

Then she leapt into the bed and pulled the covers over her head.

In a moment or two there was a rat-tat on the front door and in came the wolf. Immediately he sprang upon the bed, intent on gobbling up the shape that he could see beneath the bedclothes.

As he did so, Huge Red Riding Hood suddenly exploded from beneath them and wrapped them all around the wolf—eiderdown and blankets and sheets—until he was completely enveloped.

Then Huge Red Riding Hood sat on him.

"Hey, wait a minute!" cried the wolf indistinctly from inside all the bedclothes. "This isn't what's meant to happen. You should be saying, 'What big eyes you have and what big ears you have and what big teeth you have' and all that stuff. And anyway I can't breathe in here."

Feebly he cried "Let me out! Let me out!" but his voice grew weaker and weaker, until at last he suffocated.

Huge Red Riding Hood got off the heap of bedclothes and unwrapped them and pulled out the dead wolf by the tail. Then she dumped him outside in the garden.

"It's OK, Gran," she said, unlocking the door of the cupboard. "You can come out now."

But when her grandmother came out of the cupboard, all she said was, "Whatever have you been doing with my bed? What an awful mess it's in!"

Then she looked in the basket that her granddaughter had brought.

"It's empty!" she cried. "You horrible child! You lock me in a cupboard, you make a filthy mess of my bed, and to top it all, you've wolfed all the goodies in the basket! What a way to treat your poor old granny! I never want to see you again. Get out!"

Huge Red Riding Hood got out. As she went down the garden path, she gently prodded the body of the wolf with her huge foot.

"Sorry, old chap," said Huge Red Riding Hood. "I should have let you eat her."

HUMPTY DUMPTY

Upon a rather wobbly wall
Fat Humpty Dumpty sat;
It couldn't bear his weight at all
And so it fell down flat.
The soldiers riding by could see
That Humpty wasn't spoiled.
"It didn't hurt a bit," said he,
For Humpty was hard-boiled.

JACK SPRAT

Jack Sprat would eat no fat,
His wife would eat no lean,
So both turned vegetarian
And lived on peas and beans.

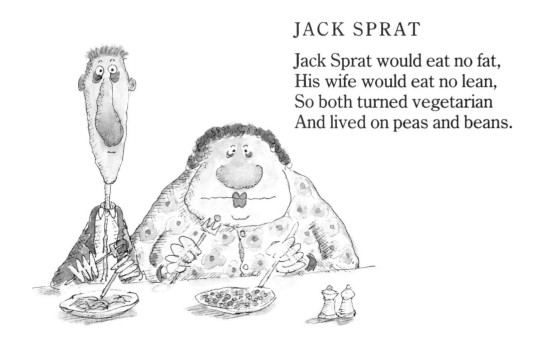

LITTLE JACK HORNER

Little Jack Horner
Sat in a corner,
Wolfing his Christmas pud;
Then he bolted his brother's,
His dad's and his mother's,
And said "I'm not feeling so good."

THE PRINCESS AND THE P
(FOR PUMPKIN)

There was once a Prince who wanted to get married. However, being a bit of a snob, he only wanted to marry a Princess. He travelled the world looking for a suitable one, but all the Princesses he met were such wimps, so precious and delicate, so *sensitive*.

"A namby-pamby lot they were, Mum," he said to the Queen on his return home. "I want a girl who can stand up for herself, a girl who can take the rough with the smooth."

"Maybe you'd better marry a commoner then," said the Queen.

"Not on your life," said the Prince.

Just then a great storm broke, and through the noise of the thunder they could hear someone banging on the palace doors.

The King went to open them, and in came a soaking wet girl.

"Jolly weather!" she cried with a merry laugh, and she shook herself like a dog, spattering them all with water.

She was a big strong handsome girl, the Prince could see.

"Are you," he said, "by any chance a Princess?"

"As a matter of fact I am," she replied, "and a jolly wet one at that."

"You'll catch your death of cold," said the Queen. "You'd better stay the night. I'll make up a bed for you."

She looks the right kind of girl, she said to herself, but we'd better find out how *sensitive* she is.

So she took all the clothes off the bed in the guest room, and then she put a pea on the bare bedstead. On top of the pea she put several mattresses and quilts, and on top of all that lot the Princess (after a nice hot bath) went to bed.

Later the Queen sneaked in to have a look but the Princess was fast asleep. So the Queen took out the pea and slipped in a lemon.

Several times more the Queen came back but each time the Princess was snoring her head off, while the Queen kept changing what was underneath all the mattresses and the quilts. She changed the lemon for a grapefruit and the grapefruit for a melon and the melon for a vegetable marrow. Finally the Queen staggered in with the largest pumpkin she could find. An enormous pumpkin it was, that anyone who was in the very least *sensitive* would have felt beneath her, no matter how many mattresses and quilts covered it, but it made no difference.

"One thing's sure, my boy," she said to the Prince at breakfast next morning. "This Princess is not a wimp, not precious or delicate, not in the very slightest bit *sensitive*. She's got a hide as thick as a rhinoceros."

Just then the Princess appeared.

"How did you sleep?" asked the Queen.

"Like a log," said the Princess.

"Want some breakfast?" said the King.

"I could eat a horse," said the Princess.

"Care to marry me?" said the Prince.

"Smashing idea!" cried the Princess, and she gave the Prince such a hearty slap on the back that his eyes filled with tears.

"Bless him!" she said to the King and the Queen. "He's so *sensitive*!"

HANSEL AND GRETEL

Once there were two children, brother and sister, and very unlucky children they were.

First, they had a perfectly horrible mother and a weak wimpish father.

Second, there was a terrible famine in the land so that no one had enough to eat.

And third, their horrible mother said to her husband, "We can't feed four mouths, but we might still be able to feed two. Let's get rid of the kids," and their father was too weak and wimpish to say no.

So Hansel and Gretel were dumped in the depths of a forest in the middle of winter, and left to die—of cold and starvation.

Tragic, eh? Imagine the poor mites, lying in the snow, clasped in each other's little arms, waiting for Death.

Forget it. Hansel and Gretel were made of sterner stuff.

Disregarding the bitter cold, they set off hand in hand through the forest, not after their parents—they'd had enough of them—but in the opposite direction, and before long they came upon a dear little cottage among the trees.

Hurrying nearer, they found that the cottage was made, not of bricks and mortar, but, would you believe it, of bread and cakes, with windows of sugar.

They did not know that inside this cottage lived a sweet old white-haired apple-cheeked lady who was actually a wicked witch.

She had the most horrible habit. She ate children.

Hansel and Gretel, being terribly hungry, set about eating bits of the cottage.

Hansel had pulled off a piece of the roof and Gretel had smashed a window when out came the witch.

"Ha! Ha!" she cackled. "You're just in time for my evening meal."

"Oh good!" they said. "We're starving. What's for supper?"

"You are," said the witch. "The oven's nice and hot, all ready for you."

Hansel and Gretel looked at one another.

"I think she's a caliban," said Hansel.

"What's that?" said Gretel.

"Someone who eats people."

"Raw?"

"No, cooked."

"Oh," said Gretel. "Why do calibans eat people?"

"Because they're hungry."

"Oh," said Gretel. "We're hungry."

Hansel looked admiringly at his little sister.

"Gretel," he said, "you aren't just a pretty face. Come on!" and between them the children dragged the wicked witch inside, and smeared her all over with lard, and shoved her in her own oven.

Later, when they'd eaten as much witch as they could manage and put the rest out in the snow to keep, they polished off the cottage for afters.

JACK AND JILL

Jack and Jill
Went up the hill
To fetch a pail of water.
Said Jack "I'm hot,
"I'll drink the lot."
Said Jill "You didn't oughter.
"'Twill make you ill,
"You'll catch a chill."
Said Jack "You make me tired."
But Jill was right.
That very night
Her brother Jack expired.

MARY HAD A LITTLE LAMB

Mary had a little lamb,
Its fleas did bite her so,
And everywhere that Mary went,
She itched from head to toe.

DIDDLE DIDDLE DUMPLING

Diddle diddle dumpling, my son John
Went to bed with his wellies on;
Down to the farmyard he had gone,
Capered in the cowpats, my son John.

SIMPLE SIMON

Simple Simon
Met a pieman
Going to the fair.
Cried Simon "Hi!
"I want a pie!"
The pieman said "Beware!
"These pies cost three
"Pounds each, you see.
"That's well beyond your range."
Said Simon "I've a
"Nice new fiver—
"You can keep the change."

GEORGE WASHINGTON

There was once a little American boy called George Washington.

A good little boy he was, always doing as he was told, always speaking politely to his elders, always—especially—telling the truth. If ever George Washington did do something a little bit naughty, so that his father had to question him about it, he would always answer truthfully.

"George," Mr Washington might say, "there are dirty footmarks all over the carpet. Did you make them, my boy?" and little George would reply, "Father, I cannot tell a lie. With my muddy boots I made them."

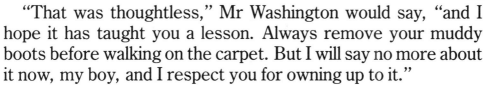

"That was thoughtless," Mr Washington would say, "and I hope it has taught you a lesson. Always remove your muddy boots before walking on the carpet. But I will say no more about it now, my boy, and I respect you for owning up to it."

However, in 1740, when George Washington was eight years old, it so happened that he was given a little axe for his birthday. Boys will be boys of course, and George looked about for something to try his new present on.

Then, in the garden, he came upon a newly-planted tree. A fine young cherry-tree it was, tall and slender, and George Washington could not resist the temptation. Swinging his little axe lustily, he chopped the cherry-tree down.

Mr Washington, you won't be surprised to hear, was not at all pleased about this, and he summoned George to his study.

"George my boy," he said. "Someone has cut down my

newly-planted young cherry-tree. What do you know of this?"

"Father," said George, "I cannot tell a lie. With my little axe I did it."

"That was thoughtless," Mr Washington said, "and I hope it has taught you a lesson. Never cut down newly-planted young cherry-trees with your little axe. But I will say no more about it now, my boy, and I respect you for owning up to it."

"Thank you, Father," said George Washington.

"I always tell the truth," he added.

"In fact," he said, "you may as well know now, Father, that one day I am going to be President."

"President?" said Mr Washington. "President of what?"

"Of America," said George Washington. "I am going to be the first President of the United States of America."

"You wicked little liar!" cried Mr Washington, and he gave his son a good shaking.

SNOW-WHITE

There was once a King whose wife gave birth to a baby daughter.

Unfortunately the poor woman then died, so that the baby, whose name was Snow-White, was left motherless.

She was called Snow-White because she was a pasty-faced baby, with no hint of colour in her cheeks.

After some years the King married again. The new Queen was enormously fat and proud of it, and she took an immediate dislike to Snow-White who was by now a very plump child and putting on weight at quite a rate.

Angrily the Queen stood in front of her mirror (a magic one, by the way) and said:

"Mirror, mirror on the wall.
Who is the fattest one of all?"

and the mirror (which always told the truth) replied:

"Lady Queen, you are the fattest one of all."

But as time passed, Snow-White grew not only taller but thicker and wider as well, and when the Queen next asked the mirror:

"Mirror, mirror on the wall.
Who is the fattest one of all?"

the mirror replied:

"To say it's you would not be right.
The fattest one is now Snow-White."

At this Snow-White's wicked stepmother became so angry that she ordered her huntsman to take Snow-White out into the forest and there do away with her.

"She's as fat as a pig," she said, "so you can kill her, and then bring me back her lungs and her liver. I'll have 'em for supper."

But out in the forest the huntsman couldn't bring himself to shove his knife through all those layers of blubber, so he told Snow-White to get lost. Then he caught a real pig, a wild forest hog, and killed it, and took its lungs and liver back to the Queen.

She ordered them to be fried, and then she covered them with dollops of blood-red tomato sauce and scoffed the lot. Afterwards she got upon the scales and saw with pleasure that she had gained a couple of pounds.

Snow-White, meanwhile, had stumbled upon a funny little house in the depths of the forest. Its front door was much too small for a big fat girl like her and she broke it off its hinges while getting in. Inside was a little table with seven little plates of food and seven little mugs of drink.

As usual, Snow-White was hungry, so she sat down, smashing the seven little chairs one after another, and ate all the food and drank all the drink. Then she felt sleepy, so she pushed together all the seven little beds that were ranged along one wall, and lay down on them. They all broke.

After dark the seven dwarfs whose house this was returned from their work as miners, and lit seven little lamps, and saw what had happened.

"The front door's bust," said the first dwarf.

"So are all our chairs," said the second dwarf.

"And all our food's gone," said the third.

"And all our drink," said the fourth.

"And all our beds are broken," said the fifth.

"Thanks to that great fat lump of a girl who's sleeping on them," said the sixth.

"Come on, boys," said the seventh dwarf. "Let's teach her a lesson."

So the seven dwarfs grabbed hold of Snow-White with their fourteen little hands, and between them dragged her away (for though they were small, they were strong), and dumped her down an old mineshaft.

Luckily there were some pools of water at the bottom of the shaft, otherwise Snow-White would have died of thirst, but there was nothing to eat and so she rapidly became much thinner.

Thus it was that when the Queen next addressed her magic mirror, saying as usual:

"Mirror, mirror on the wall.
Who is the fattest one of all?"

the mirror replied:

"You are the fattest one around,
For now Snow-White is underground."

Then the Queen was sure that Snow-White was dead.

"Not that I doubted it," she said to herself. "She wouldn't have got far without her lungs and her liver."

But in fact before long Snow-White was rescued.

A young Prince, hunting in the forest, heard her faint cries for help from the bottom of the mineshaft. He let down a rope and pulled her up—fairly easily for now she was quite a pretty shape. And the Prince fell in love with her on the spot as princes do, and took her home, and married her.

He would have done better to wait a bit, because now Snow-White was so hungry that she spent every hour of the day eating. Soon she was even fatter than she had ever been, and

the poor Prince found himself with a pasty-faced wife who thought of nothing but food and was disgustingly greedy.

Meanwhile, back at the palace, the Queen could not break herself of the habit of consulting the magic mirror.

"Mirror, mirror on the wall.
Who is the fattest one of all?"

she asked with a smug smile on her face.
But the mirror replied:

"Snow-White's the fattest. She's not dead
But to a handsome Prince is wed.
She's fatter than she's ever been,
So eat your heart out, Lady Queen."

On hearing these words, Snow-White's wicked stepmother promptly died of a broken heart.

As for Snow-White and her handsome Prince, they both lived unhappily ever after.

KING CANUTE

King Canute ruled over three countries. He became King of England in 1016, of Denmark in 1019, and of Norway in 1028.

Perhaps it was the strain of having three crowns to wear, but it all went to his head, and he began to think of himself as almost god-like.

"There's nothing in the world I cannot do if I set my mind to it," he told his courtiers, and they knew better than to argue. Someone did say, "You can't fly," but he said it very quietly.

From then on King Canute became much too big for his boots, and at court everybody secretly thought that it would be nice to take him down a peg or two. But no one dared.

Until at last, on a fine summer's day, the perfect opportunity arose.

The whole court had gone for a day out at the seaside, taking a picnic, and when they reached the sands they stood at the head of the beach, watching the waves breaking. The tide was coming in, and the ripples moved slowly up the beach, each wave reaching just a little higher than the last.

"Just look at my sea," said King Canute, for by now he was so swollen-headed that he thought he ruled the world.

"Your sea is indeed beautiful, Sire," said one courtier.

"And powerful, like Your Majesty," said another.

"See how the waves reach relentlessly further and further up the beach," said a third. "Nothing could turn them back."

"I could," said King Canute. "Easy as winking."

The courtiers looked at one another. He's gone over the top this time, they thought. Turn the waves back! No one could possibly do that! And one of them, seeing this opportunity, said, "Pray show us your power, Sire. Command the mighty sea to go back."

"No problem," said King Canute. "Fetch my throne."

So they brought the portable throne that always travelled to the seaside in the back of the royal ox-wagon, along with all the picnic things, and set it down where the King indicated, at the top of the beach, by a line of seaweed and driftwood on the sand.

The advancing tide was now no more than twenty yards away, and the courtiers waited expectantly for the King to command the waves to go back. They wouldn't of course! They were getting nearer by the minute. No man could turn them back. What a fool the King would look!

They waited and waited but King Canute did not speak. He simply sat on his portable throne, wiggling his toes in the sand and looking smug.

Then at long last, when the highest ripple of all reached the line of seaweed and driftwood, the King cried in a loud voice, "I, Canute, King of England, of Denmark and of Norway, command my waves to go back!"

And so they did, for the tide had turned.

The courtiers stood speechless, watching the water receding.

Then a voice broke the silence.

"Told you so," said King Canute.

MARY, MARY

Mary, Mary, quite contrary,
How does your garden grow?
It's nothing to do
With nosy old you,
So mind your own business and go.

LITTLE BO-PEEP

Little Bo-Peep
Has lost her sheep.
She's terribly down on her luck,
And well might she cry
For the rustlers came by
And drove them away in a truck.

THE FROG KING

Once there was a Princess (beautiful of course) whose favourite toy was a ball (a gold one, naturally) which (because I suppose she couldn't think of anything better to do) she liked to play with by throwing up into the air and catching again.

One day she was doing this beside a well, when she missed (butterfingers) and the ball dropped into the well and sank.

Whereupon (being a thoroughly spoiled little miss) she began to stamp her feet and bawl her eyes out.

Just then a croaky voice (yes, you've guessed, it was a frog) said, "Oi, you! Why are you making all that fuss?"

"I dropped my, boo-hoo, gold ball into the, boo-hoo, well," sobbed the Princess.

"Well, what will you, ribbit-ribbit, give me if I, ribbit-ribbit, fetch it out for you?" said the frog.

"Anything you like!" cried the Princess. "My jewels, my pearls, my dresses—anything."

"No fear," said the frog. "That's not my scene. But if you will love me, and let me sit beside you at table and eat off your golden plate and drink from your mug, then I'll go down and fetch your rotten old ball."

The frog, you see, (you knew it all the time, didn't you?) was actually a handsome young King who'd got on the wrong side of a witch. Only the kindness of a Princess could change him back again.

The Princess dried her tears.

"OK frog," she said. "It's a deal."

So the Frog King dived down into the well and fetched the gold ball. Then the princess carried him home.

Once inside the palace the Princess took the Frog King straight down to the kitchens. Here she gave orders to the Head Cook. Then she came out, without the Frog King.

When all the other members of her family came into the banqueting hall for supper that evening, the Princess had already started her meal (by the way, I forgot to tell you she was a French Princess).

The others looked at what was on the Princess's golden plate.

"Qu'est-ce que tu manges?" they asked.

("What are you eating?")

And the Princess replied:

"Les cuisses de grenouille."

("Frog's legs.")

ROBIN HOOD AND HIS
MISERABLE MEN

Long long ago, in Sherwood Forest in the county of Nottinghamshire, there lived a man who was known as Robin Hood, probably because he liked robin people.

He had a wife called Maid Marian, probably because Robin made her keen on marian him.

Maid Marian had a great many sisters, so that Robin acquired a whole lot of brothers-in-law, who became known as the Inlaws, and a miserable lot of fellows they were.

You can't blame them really, because they had no roof over their heads in Sherwood Forest and most of the time it rained, and often it was bitterly cold, except sometimes in summertime and even then the trees were so thick they didn't see much of the sun.

What's more, they didn't have much to eat except for nuts and berries, because although the forest was full of deer, all the Inlaws were such rotten shots. They shot at the deer like mad with their longbows, but though the arrows flew everywhere, into bushes and tree trunks and sometimes into other Inlaws, they hardly ever hit a deer.

Actually Robin Hood was the worst bowman of them all. A skinny weakly little chap, he could never draw the bowstring tight enough to send the arrow any distance.

Even when someone did manage to kill a deer, usually either a very young or a very old one, most of the band didn't get much of it, because two of the Inlaws got the lion's share.

One was a giant of a man called Little John, and the other was a very fat and greedy priest named Friar Tuck. Little John used to biff the other Inlaws with a great pole called a quarterstaff to keep them away, and then he and Friar Tuck would gorge themselves while Robin Hood and his Miserable Men stood around in the rain, hoping for scraps.

Poor old Robin Hood, he led a wretched life.

Most of the time he was wet and cold and hungry.

None of his Miserable Men, like Will Scarlet or Allan A'Dale or Much the miller's son, thought anything of him.

Little John and Friar Tuck ate all the grub.

Maid Marian gave him a hard time.

And finally the Sheriff of Nottingham and his men were forever chasing about in the forest trying to catch Robin Hood. They needn't really have bothered, because he was a most unsuccessful robber. He had the idea, you see, that it was his mission in life to rob the poor to feed the rich, but of course the poor people he stole from never had two pennies to rub together.

Saddest of all was his end.

As he lay dying (of exposure, starvation, double pneumonia and a broken heart), he said to Maid Marian, "Bring me my bow."

"Whatever for?" she said.

"I will shoot an arrow," said Robin Hood, "and wherever it falls, there bury me."

All the Miserable Men, the whole band of Inlaws, were standing around, and they heard these words.

"One thing's sure," said Will Scarlet. "We shan't have far to carry him."

"Too true," said Allan A'Dale. "He never could shoot any distance."

"And he certainly won't be able to now," said Much the miller's son.

"I might as well dig the grave right next to him," said Little John, and so he did.

Then the Inlaws helped poor old Robin fit an arrow to his bowstring.

He pulled it feebly and the arrow plopped straight into the grave.

Exhausted by the effort, Robin Hood died.

"Bless him," said Friar Tuck, as they tipped the body in.

Little John leaned on his quarterstaff and looked down reflectively at the skinny little corpse.

"Poor old chap," he said. "He never amounted to anything when he was alive. Why don't we make sure he does now that he's dead?"

"What d'you mean?" asked the other Inlaws.

"Well," said Little John, "let's spread the story that Robin Hood was really a hero—a marvellous bowman, a wonderful fighter feared by all his enemies, especially the Sheriff of Nottingham, and loved and admired by all his Miserable Men."

"Merry Men would be better," said Friar Tuck.

"And if we tell enough people," went on Little John, "then in time everyone will come to believe that was what Robin Hood was really like."

So that's what they did.

ROCK-A-BYE, BABY

Rock-a-bye, baby, on the tree top.
Oh, that the horrible baby would stop!
The ugly great creature's so heavy and fat
The poor little tree's going to fall over flat.

RING-A-RING O' ROSES

Ring-a-ring o' roses,
You've all got runny noses.
Goodness, how I loathe 'em.
Don't you ever blow them?
Atishoo! Atishoo!
Is all I hear all day.
I don't want your sniffly colds.
Sneeze the other way.

THE SLEEPING BEAUTY

Everyone knows the story of the Sleeping Princess.

How twelve jolly nice fairies were invited to her christening, but the thirteenth, a smelly old toe-rag, wasn't. And how the old toe-rag was niggled at not being asked, and so promised that, at the age of fifteen, the Princess would prick her finger with a needle and die.

And how the twelfth (jolly nice) fairy said, "No, she won't, she'll just fall into a deep sleep for a hundred years."

Well, you'd have thought the Princess would have had the sense to steer clear of needles, but no, at the age of fifteen the silly creature had to come across an aged woman (any fool should have known it was the old toe-rag) and have a go on her spinning-wheel, and prick her finger, and KER-ZONK! she was out like a light.

Everyone knows too that the inhabitants of the Palace also fell asleep at that precise moment. The King, the Queen, the courtiers, the servants, the animals—every one of them dropped off, no matter what they were doing.

Cooks stirring soup, serving-wenches sweeping floors, gardeners digging, bakers baking, butlers butling, flunkeys flunking, ostlers ostling, and turnspits turning spits—each fell fast asleep in the middle of whatever he or she was doing. The Queen's little pet dog in fact had his leg cocked, all ready to sprinkle the white-stockinged leg of the Chamberlain of the Royal Household, but both were instantly in slumberland before any damage could be done.

Everyone knows all this stuff, but what no one knows is exactly what happened a hundred years later.

I don't mean the bit about a Prince hearing the story of the Sleeping Beauty, and making his way through the terrible thorn-hedge that had grown up around the Palace. Nor the part where he finds all the inhabitants snoring their heads off.

I mean when he actually reached the Princess's bedchamber, and stared down at her sleeping figure and saw how beautiful she was. OK so he kissed her and she woke up.

And so did the King and the Queen and all the court, and the cooks started stirring again, the serving-wenches swept, the gardeners dug, the bakers baked, the butlers butled, the flunkeys flunked, the ostlers ostled, and the turnspits turned their spits. And the Queen's little pet dog made a pretty design all down the Chamberlain of the Royal Household's white-stockinged leg.

But up in the bedchamber the Princess gave the Prince one heck of a smack in the face.

"I don't know who you think you are," she said, "but you've got a flipping nerve, barging into a girl's room and waking her up. I need my beauty sleep."

"But . . . but . . . but," stammered the Prince, "I thought you wanted waking up. You've been asleep for a hundred years."

"A hundred years!" said the Princess. "You must be joking! What d'you think this is—a fairy story?"

I LOVE LITTLE PUSSY

I hate little pussy
For making me sneeze.
Whenever she's near me
I sniff and I wheeze.

So I shoo her away
And I shout at her "Scat!"
I'm allergic to pussy,
The hairy old cat.